INSECTS

Tina Glendadakis

Illustrated By:
Dwight Nacaytuna

Copyright © 2023 **Tina's Publishing**

All rights reserved. No part of this publication may be reproduced, distributed, or transmitted in any form or by any means, including photocopying, recording, or other electronic or mechanical methods, without the prior written permission of the publisher, except in the case of brief quotations embodied in critical reviews and certain other noncommercial uses permitted by copyright law. For permission requests, write to the publisher, addressed "Attention: Book Rights and Permission," at the address below.

Published in the United States of America

ISBN 978-1-962110-59-4 (SC)

Tina's Publishing
222 West 6th Street
Suite 400, San Pedro, CA, 90731
tglendadakis@hotmail.com

Order Information and Rights Permission:

Quantity sales. Special discounts might be available on quantity purchases by corporations, associations, and others. For details, contact the publisher at the address above.

For Book Rights Adaptation and other Rights Permission.
Call us at toll-free 1-888-945-8513 or send us an email at admin@stellarliterary.com.

INSECTS

Big and small

They creep up your wall.

Others, still, lurk down the hall.

Never watching where to go

Careful! They may climb on your toe.

Never watching what to do

Careful! They may eat your stew.

Smiling, gliding, here and there

They make double trouble everywhere!

Who knows what they eat.

Do you think it's wheat?

Are they really neat?

Do they ever weep?

And if they sleep, is it deep?

Do they all keep moving?

Or stop to have a seat?

Do they sit on their feet?

There are some that like to stick on you.
But beware of those that pick on you
'cause peek-a-boo, they're chasing you
And you'll have to flee, like a honey bee.

Ring a ding-ding
Watch out for a sting!

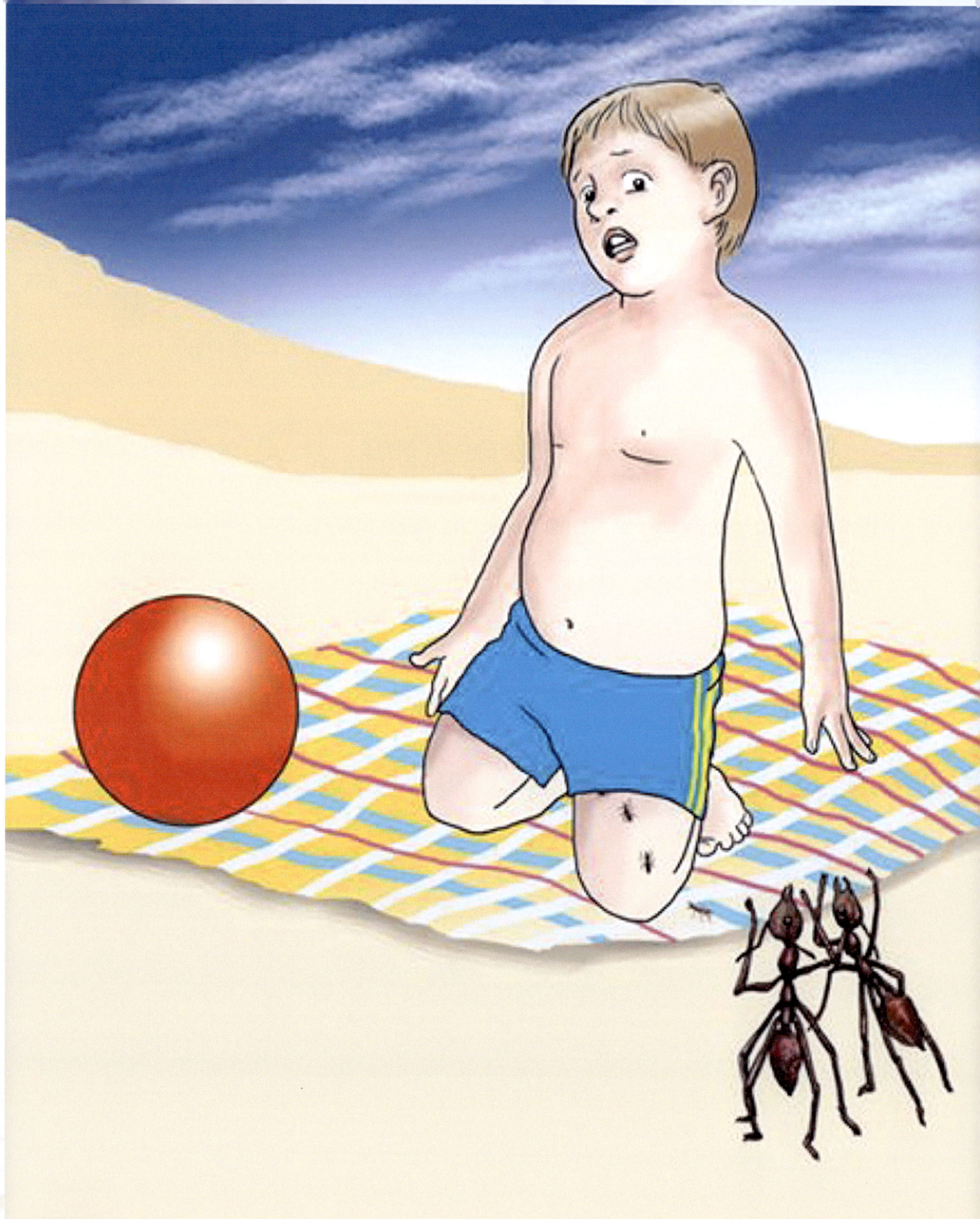

When you play with insects in the sand

Soon enough, they'll be crawling up your pants.

And you might wiggle 'cause it tickles!

But please don't do a dance or the ants will dance with you!

Insects have a secret code of how to break into a home.

And as they roam in your home

They won't steal, only feel

All the things that appeal to their eyes as they spy

Don't be scared, they're your friends.

Do not mope, hope for more.

You can cope with a bunch

And I have a hunch they will eat your lunch

With a munch, munch, munch, munch, munch.

Out on the farm the cops

Arrest them for eating the crops.

When they go to jail

They have to mop

So hard they slowly start to drop.

Of if the weather's nice and hot

They go sweep the lot.

Then rest awhile to drink some pop

But the fizz has them hop to the top

Looking like dots.

Oops! Better hope not!

Insects love the bright light

And stay until night.

Flying to the ceiling

Cause they're not scared of heights.

Sometimes they will fight for the light

Until at last they see a kite

And fly away with great delight.

White with fright, they hold on tight.

Oh yes I'm right

It's quite a sight!

Insects love to ride upon a bus

Needing a few more cents

They start feeling tense.

How on earth, are they so dense?

Never quite realizing in all this fuss...

They just missed the bus!

What a pity

They love to see the city.

So when you see those insects flying, crawling, here and there
Don't rush off to crush them.
Just brush them off to hush them!

Printed by Libri Plureos GmbH in Hamburg, Germany